The Case of the
Stinky Science Project

Read all the Jigsaw Jones Mysteries

The Case of the
Stinky Science Project

by James Preller
illustrated by John Speirs
cover illustration by R. W. Alley

A
LITTLE APPLE
PAPERBACK

SCHOLASTIC INC.
New York Toronto London Auckland Sydney
Mexico City New Delhi Hong Kong

For the wonderful, fantastic, fabulous, stupendous kids at
Hamagrael Elementary!
—J. P.

Book design by Dawn Adelman

ISBN 0-439-11428-4

12 11 10 9 8 7 6 5 4 3 2 1   0 1 2 3 4 5/0

Printed in the U.S.A.
First Scholastic printing, March 2000

CONTENTS

Chapter One

Sally-Ann Simms

The pink bows didn't fool me. I ignored the matching lace socks and the little red plastic pocketbook. I knew that Sally-Ann Simms was one tough cookie.

So what if she was only four and a half years old.

Sally-Ann stood in my backyard, hands on her hips. She shouted up to my tree house, "Jigsaw Jones! You up there?"

I was up there — and I told her so. "Take the ladder," I called down. "The elevator's broken."

Sally-Ann scooted up the ladder. "Your sister, Hillary, said I could find you here," Sally-Ann said.

I held out a paper cup. "Grape juice?" I offered.

Sally-Ann sat down, cross-legged. She grabbed the cup and drained it, slurping loudly. A purple mustache formed over her upper lip. Eyes wide, she looked around. "It's nice up here. It feels like I'm in a bird's nest."

"My dad built it," I explained. "It's kind of wobbly. But he promises it won't fall down." I rapped on a wall with my knuckles. "I hope he's right."

Sally-Ann fished in her little red pocketbook. She pulled out a windup Tarzan toy. She carefully placed it in front of me. "I talked to Wingnut O'Brien," Sally-Ann began. "He said you could help me."

I smiled. "Yeah, good old Wingnut. I found his lost hamster a while back. For a dollar a day, I make problems go away." I frowned at Sally-Ann's empty cup. "More grape juice?"

She nodded. "I don't have much money," Sally-Ann said.

"How much is *not much*, exactly?" I asked.

Sally-Ann fidgeted with her lace socks. "Zero dollars and zero cents."

You didn't need a calculator to do the math. I picked up the Tarzan toy. It was the

kind you get for free with a Happy Meal. One of his arms was missing. "And you hope to pay me . . . *with this*?" I asked. I handed Tarzan back to her. "Sorry, but I've got enough broken toys."

Sally-Ann stared into my eyes. She sighed and got up to leave. That's when I knew I was going to take the case. For free. I just couldn't say no to eyes like that.

Here's the thing. Sally-Ann Simms might have been four feet tall — if she stood on a box and jumped. And the little squirt needed help. *My* help.

Jigsaw Jones, Private Eye.

I reached for Tarzan again. "I guess he's okay," I said. "Let me get my partner. Then you can tell us both all about your problem."

"Thanks, Jigsaw," Sally-Ann said. "I'm sorry I don't have any money. It's just . . ."

"Just . . . what?" I asked.

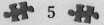

"It's just that . . . I had to give my ice-cream money to Bobby Solofsky," Sally-Ann said.

I chewed on that for a minute. It left a bad taste in my mouth. Yeah, I thought. Solofsky's just the type to take Popsicle money from a four-year-old.

Chapter Two

Tricked!

Mila Yeh was my best friend and partner. Always had been. She worked with me on all the tough cases. The easy ones, too. She hurried over when I called.

We could hear Mila singing from around the house. Mila was *always* singing something. But she usually changed the words. Today, she was singing "Yellow Submarine" by the Beatles, sort of:

"We all live in a purple submarine, purple submarine, purple submarine."

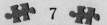 7

Mila bent over, picked up a rock, and hurled it at a tree. *Bull's-eye!* She began singing again:

"We all swim in a washing machine, washing machine, washing machine."

"Hi, guys," Mila said, greeting us. She sprawled on the tree house floor and poured herself a cup of grape juice.

"Help yourself," I offered.

"Thanks," Mila replied, beaming. "I just did." She looked at me. "So what's up?"

"We were waiting for you," I said. "Something about Bobby Solofsky."

Mila turned to Sally-Ann. "Solofsky, huh? We've had trouble with him before. Can you tell me what happened?"

"Bobby tricked me and took my ice-cream money," Sally-Ann declared. "I want it back!"

Mila gently placed her hand on Sally-Ann's shoulder. "What do you mean, he tricked you?" she asked.

Sally-Ann seemed upset. I offered her a box of Kleenex. I thought it was a nice thing to do. Sally-Ann didn't see it that way.

"I'm not a crybaby," Sally-Ann scoffed.

"Sure," I said. "I just thought . . ."

Sally-Ann glared at me. "Don't treat me like a baby," she said. "Just get my money back!"

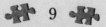

She was something, that Sally-Ann
Simms. A walking hurricane in lavender
and pink.

I opened my detective journal to a clean
page. Using bright pink marker in honor of
Sally-Ann's lace socks, I wrote: **Client: Sally-
Ann Simms.**

"I'm all ears," I said.

Sally began, "I was having a tea party
with Mr. Bear and Lady Snuggles and . . ."

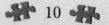

"*Lady Snuggles?*" I asked.

Sally-Ann fixed me with a stare. "Yeah, Lady Snuggles. My stuffed doll. You got a problem with that?"

I stammered, "No, er, I just . . ."

"You just . . . *what*?" Sally-Ann asked sharply.

"Never mind," I said. "What happened next?"

"Bobby came by," she said, turning to

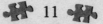

Mila. "He was bragging that he had magical powers."

Mila raised an eyebrow. "Magical powers? Bobby Solofsky?"

Sally-Ann nodded. "I didn't believe him, either. Then he took out a book and a balloon."

I held up my hand. "What color balloon?"

"Red, I think," Sally-Ann said. "Who cares?"

"I do," I said. "It may be a clue. Was the balloon blown up?"

"No, it was . . . *un-blown up*," Sally-Ann remembered. "He said he could move the book with just a balloon."

"Don't tell me you bet him," I said.

Sally-Ann cast her eyes downward. I had my answer. "It's the oldest trick in town," I explained. "He used air pressure to lift the book."

Sally-Ann shook her head. "I don't know

about that. He just put the balloon under the book and blew it up."

Mila spoke up. "The book moved and you had to pay up."

Sally-Ann nodded unhappily.

After Sally-Ann left, Mila and I talked about the case. "It doesn't look good," I said. "It was a fair bet."

"I *suppose*," Mila said. "But it's still a rotten trick. Sally-Ann's not even in kindergarten."

I scribbled a quick picture in my journal. It showed a blown-up balloon underneath a book. Too bad it turned out looking like a fish wearing a bad hat. "I'll have a talk with

Bobby in school tomorrow," I told her. "But I don't think it will do much good."

"You'll figure out something," Mila said. "You always do." She climbed down the ladder and skipped away, singing:

*"We all live in a yellow marshmallow,
yellow marshmallow, yellow
marshmallow!"*

Chapter Three

Mila's Secret Code

I sat next to Mila on the school bus Monday morning.

She leaned close to my ear. "I made up a new code last night." Mila liked to test my brainpower with secret codes.

"Great," I said. "Hand it over."

"This one is a brain buster!" Mila warned. "It might make your head *explode*."

"Try me," I offered.

She handed me a piece of paper torn from a notepad.

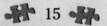

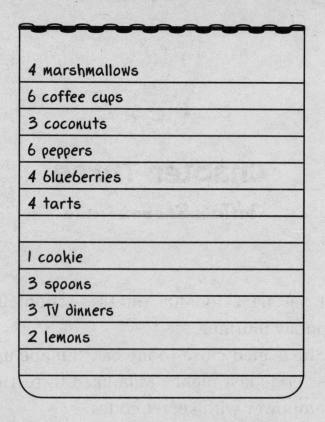

4 marshmallows

6 coffee cups

3 coconuts

6 peppers

4 blueberries

4 tarts

1 cookie

3 spoons

3 TV dinners

2 lemons

"I think you made a mistake, Mila," I said. "This looks like a shopping list."

Mila smiled. "I know it *looks* like a shopping list. You've got to look harder," she said.

I stared at the list for a long time. I had to admit it. I was bamboozled.

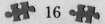

"Do you need a hint?" Mila asked.

I frowned. "I'll figure it out," I said. I didn't want Mila to get the best of me. I studied the code some more. It sure made a strange shopping list. I mean, who buys only four marshmallows? And why would someone want just three spoons? It didn't make any sense.

I shoved the note in my pocket.

"Give up?" Mila asked.

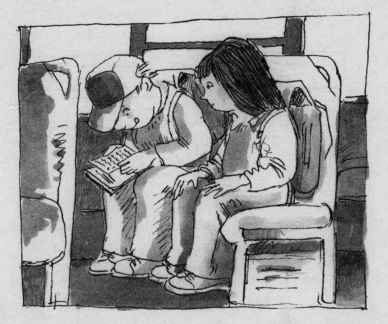

"No, I don't give up," I replied. "But this one might take a little time. My brain needs a rest. Besides," I told her, "you don't really want my head to explode, do you?"

Mila shook her head. "Nah. Too messy."

I opened my detective journal. I drew a self-portrait. It showed my head exploding into pieces. It was a pretty good picture, even though the lines were wobbly. Drawing on a bus isn't the easiest thing in the world.

I showed Mila the picture. It made her laugh. "Definitely too messy," she said.

We heard loud laughter from the back of the bus. It was Bobby Solofsky. He was

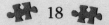

horsing around with Eddie Becker and Mike Radcliffe.

"Do you want me to talk to Bobby?" Mila asked.

I shook my head. "I'll do it," I said. "Later on. I've already got one headache this morning. I don't need another."

The bus dropped us off at school. I stuffed the journal in my backpack. Meantime, I kept wondering about that code. Four marshmallows? Two lemons?

Four blueberries? What could someone cook with four blueberries? Maybe that was the trick. Maybe the list was a recipe for something.

Oh, brother.

I knew that my head couldn't explode. Not really. But just in case, I pulled my baseball cap down tight. Yeesh. This time, Mila was *really* testing my brainpower!

Chapter Four

The Volcano

There was a big crowd gathered by the front doors. Helen Zuckerman, Geetha Nair, and Danika Starling were carrying . . . *a mountain!*

"Outta the way!" hollered Helen. "Coming through!"

Mila and Ralphie Jordan held open the doors.

"What's that?" asked Athena Lorenzo.

"Our science project," Helen said.

Ralphie looked worried. "Science project?! Did you say *science project*?!

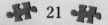

Uh-oh — I knew I should pay more attention in class. Nobody told *me* about any science projects!"

Geetha laughed. "Don't worry, Ralphie. This is our independent project. We did it for extra credit."

Ralphie wiped his hand across his forehead. "Whew!" he exclaimed. The smile returned to his face. "But why did you build a mountain?"

"It's a volcano," Helen corrected him.

That got us all buzzing. A volcano — awesome. Everybody loved volcanoes. Besides, we'd been talking about them in class.

"Will it spew hot lava?" Bigs Maloney asked hopefully.

Danika smiled. "Just wait and see," she said in a singsongy voice. "We're going to show it to everybody in class."

Bigs took that as a definite yes. He

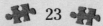

pumped his fist in the air. "All right! Hot molten lava! I can't wait!"

Our teacher, Ms. Gleason, stood in the doorway to room 201. She waved her arms. "This way, girls. Careful now. Watch out for my — *ouch!* — foot."

"Whoops! Sorry about that, Ms. Gleason," Helen apologized.

They placed the volcano on a table in the hallway. "This way, everyone can admire

it," Ms. Gleason said. We all gathered around to take a closer look.

"Please take your seats, children," Ms. Gleason said. "Tomorrow the girls will give us a little demonstration — because their volcano *really works*!"

Everyone cheered. We couldn't wait.

Unfortunately, we had to wait. But we did get to talk more about volcanoes.

"Can anyone name the three different kinds of volcanoes?" Ms. Gleason asked.

Danika Starling's hand shot up.

Ms. Gleason looked around the room. "Anyone else? We talked about this on Friday."

Danika waved her hand desperately. Ms. Gleason finally nodded in her direction.

"Active, dormant, and . . . um, extinct," Danika answered.

"Nice job, Danika," Ms. Gleason said. She wrote the words on the blackboard:

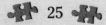

ACTIVE
DORMANT
EXTINCT

Ms. Gleason pointed to the word ACTIVE. "An active volcano may erupt at any time. There are about five hundred active volcanoes in the world," she said.

"Cool!" yelled Mike Radcliffe.

"Not exactly, Mike," Ms. Gleason replied with a smile. "Volcanoes are hot — very, very hot. The molten rock inside a volcano, called *lava*, can be two thousand degrees!"

We all thought that was pretty cool. I mean, *hot*.

"*Dormant* is another word for sleeping," Ms. Gleason told us. "A dormant volcano is sleeping. It has not erupted in a long time. Sometimes for thousands of years. But scientists think it still might one day."

She pointed to the word EXTINCT. "Can

anyone guess what an extinct volcano is like?"

Ralphie Jordan grabbed his throat and made choking noises. "It's dead!" he said. "Like the dinosaurs!"

"Wonderful, Ralphie," Ms. Gleason said. "An extinct volcano will probably never erupt again."

"Bummer!" Eddie Becker complained.

"Let's hope *our* dormant volcano will wake up tomorrow!" Ms. Gleason said. "Right, girls?"

She winked at Helen, Geetha, and Danika.

"Hot, burning lava," Bigs shouted. "Yippee!"

Chapter Five

Bobby and Yoda

In the cafeteria, I heard Bigs Maloney ask Bobby Solofsky a question. Bigs wondered, "Have you gone bonkers?"

Bobby didn't answer.

So Bigs jerked a thumb the size of a pickle toward me. "Tell him," he ordered Bobby.

Bobby made a face. "I said Spider-Man could beat Yoda in a fight."

"Yoda?" I asked. "Big ears, Jedi Master, talks like Grover from *Sesame Street*?"

Bobby nodded.

 29

"No way!" Bigs roared. "Yoda has the Force!"

"Yoda," Bobby replied, "has more wrinkles than a dried prune."

Outraged, Bigs pounded a fist on the table. The table, amazingly, didn't break in half. "Yoda would win, easy!" he said.

Bobby took a big bite of his tuna fish sandwich. I could tell it was tuna fish — because I had a good view of it. Bobby chewed with his mouth open. It wasn't a pretty sight.

"Have you ever seen him walk?" Bobby asked. "The guy's, like, nine million years old. Yoda can barely move. How could he fight?"

"Yoda is a Jedi Master!" Bigs argued. "He trained Luke Skywalker and Qui-Gon Jinn!"

Bobby just shook his head. "Have you *looked* at Yoda's arms? Have you? He couldn't lift my lunch box!"

I could see Bigs Maloney's face turn red. I

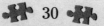

tried changing the subject. "Uh, guys," I said. "This is very interesting. But I'm on a case."

Bobby yawned. "Big deal."

I pulled out my journal. "I need to ask you a few questions, Bobby."

Bobby smirked. "Ask away," he said. "I didn't do nothing to nobody."

I looked at Bigs. "Sorry, Bigs. This is private."

Bigs shrugged and walked away. That left me alone with Bobby Solofsky. Oh, joy. "I had a visit from Sally-Ann Simms," I began. "She says you tricked her."

Bobby opened his mouth in fake surprise. "Me? Trick Sally-Ann? I won that money fair and square, *Theodore*."

He called me Theodore just to bug me. It worked. I was bugged.

Bobby continued, "I said I could make a book move by using only a balloon. I won the bet. Fair and square."

I reminded him that Sally-Ann was only four years old.

"So?" Bobby said. He had all the sympathy of a tarantula.

I sighed. "Okay, Solofsky. I guess you win. But next time, try tricking someone your own age."

Bobby folded his hands behind his head. "Sure thing, *Theodore*. Tell you what. I've been working on an amazing new magic trick. Why don't *you* bet me. If you win, I'll give Sally-Ann's money back."

"And if I lose?" I asked.

Bobby flashed a toothy smile. "I get to use your tree house — *for a whole week*."

Chapter Six

The Mysterious Floating Egg

I may have blinked. I'm not sure. The thought of Bobby Solofsky using my tree house gave me the creeps. "What's the trick?" I asked.

Bobby smiled, like a fisherman who feels a tug on the line. Now he wanted to reel me in. He said, "I can float an egg in a jar of water."

"What do you mean?" I asked. "*On* the water?"

"No, *in* the water," Bobby said. "Let me borrow a piece of paper."

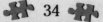 34

Bobby drew a picture of a glass jar filled with water. Right in the middle, he drew an egg. "It won't sink," he said.

"Plain drinking water?" I asked.

Bobby nodded. "Is it a bet?" His eyes twinkled with delight.

Luckily, the school bell rang. It was time to get back to class. "I'll let you know tomorrow," I told him.

Bobby tried to hide his disappointment. "Sure, *Theodore*," he said. "But I hope you bet me. I've always liked that tree house of yours."

I guess Ms. Gleason was still on her science kick. That afternoon she reminded us about the scientific method. "Remember what I told you before, when we did our experiments with mealworms," she said. "A scientist is like a detective."

My ears perked up.

She continued, "The world is full of mystery. Scientists try to discover the truth. They ask questions. They investigate. They try to learn facts. Scientists do this by using the scientific method."

Ms. Gleason handed out sheets of paper. They read:

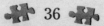

THE SCIENTIFIC METHOD

1. Identify the problem. <u>What do you want to know?</u>
2. Gather information. <u>What do you already know?</u>
3. Make a prediction. <u>What do you think will happen?</u>
4. Test the prediction. <u>Experiment!</u>
5. Draw a conclusion based on what you learned. <u>Why did the experiment work out the way it did?</u>

I decided that she was right. A scientist *was* like a detective. Only without secret disguises and invisible ink.

After school, I visited Sally-Ann Simms. I had to tell her about my talk with Bobby Solofsky. But first, Sally-Ann introduced me to her stuffed animals.

"Say hello to Mr. Bear and Lady Snuggles," she said.

I mumbled something.

Sally-Ann made a sour face. "Louder," she demanded. "Lady Snuggles can't hear you."

Maybe I said hello to Lady Snuggles. I don't exactly remember. Then I told Sally-Ann the bad news. Bobby wasn't giving the money back.

"I don't care about the money," she shot back. "You can keep the money. I just don't want Bobby to have it. He doesn't play fair."

I tried to explain that life wasn't a bowl of cherries. "I hate cherries," Sally-Ann replied. "Besides, you help *everybody*. Now help me. *Please*."

Yeesh.

I dragged myself over to Mila's.

"Jigsaw!" Mila greeted me. "Did you solve the code?"

 39

"Actually, I could use your help on something else," I said. I told her about Bobby's floating egg trick. She listened closely. "Do you think I should make the bet?"

Mila pulled on her long black hair. "Let's try it ourselves," she suggested.

We went back to my house. I found a glass jar in the kitchen closet. We filled the jar with water. I dropped an egg into the water.

Plop!

It sank like a stone.

Chapter Seven

Thinking Like a Scientist

I tried another egg.

Plop.

It sank, too.

"I have a prediction," I announced. *"Eggs don't float."*

"Maybe we should experiment some more," Mila said. "Just to test your *prediction*."

I pulled out the whole carton of eggs. Two of them dropped on the floor. *Cra-ack.*

"Gross!" Mila said. "You stepped in it."

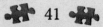

"Shhh!" I held a finger to my lips. "My mom's in the next room."

I cleaned up the mess. Most of it, anyway. The floor was still a little sticky. And so were my socks. Mila and I returned to the experiment. Every egg fell to the bottom of the jar.

"I was wondering," Mila said, rocking back and forth in her chair. "Was the egg supposed to be regular or *hard-boiled*?"

"We didn't discuss eggs," I said.

So we decided to experiment with hard-boiled eggs. After all, it's what a scientist would do. Only this time, we needed help from a grown-up.

I found my mom in the living room. She was reading a thick book. My big, lazy dog, Rags, was asleep by her feet. "Better than slippers," my dad always said.

"Hey, Mom. Could you make me a hard-boiled egg?"

She waved her hand like a magic wand. "Presto! You're a hard-boiled egg."

"Very funny, Mom," I groaned. "But could you?"

She looked up in surprise. Even Rags looked up. He seemed surprised, too. "I didn't know you *liked* hard-boiled eggs," Mom said.

"It's not to eat," I said. "We're doing an experiment."

"Uh-oh," she said. "Are you two making a mess in there?"

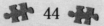

"No, honest," I said. "We're just trying to think like scientists."

"And how does a scientist think?" she asked.

I sighed. Parents, yeesh. Kids have to explain *the simplest things* to them.

"It's like this," I explained. "You have to use something called the scientific method. First you make a *hypothesis*. That's a big word. It means guess, I think. Then you test it, by *experimenting*. Then you draw a *conclusion* based on the facts."

"I see," she said. "But what does this have to do with a hard-boiled egg?"

"Please, Mom," I begged. "It's important."

My mother stood up and stretched. "Okay, kiddo. One hard-boiled egg, coming up."

"Thanks, Mom."

She bent down and gave me a quick kiss. "Sure thing, Mr. Thomas Edison. Since you asked so nicely."

 45

She even boiled *a few* eggs for us, just in case. Each one sank to the bottom. "I'm ready to draw my conclusion," I told Mila. "*Eggs definitely don't float in water.* There's no way Bobby can make an egg float."

"I *suppose* not," Mila said. "But what if Bobby pulls a fast one?"

"What can he do?" I asked. "It's just a jar, some water, and an egg. You don't really think he has magical powers, do you?"

Mila didn't answer. She just rocked back and forth. Softly, she said to herself, "Something's wrong. There's a trick to this. But I don't know what." She stood up to leave. "Gotta go, Jigsaw. Talk to you later."

"Where are you going?" I asked.

Mila smiled. "To speak with an expert."

Chapter Eight
Cracking the Code

Mila called me later that night. "It's a trick," she said. "Bobby probably puts salt in the water. Salt makes the water more dense, so things float easier."

"How do you know?" I asked.

"I talked to my father. He reminded me about our trip to Cape Cod last summer," she said.

"What does that have to do with anything?" I asked.

"We swam a lot," Mila said. "It's easy to float in the ocean. Salt water, you know."

Now I understood. "But Bobby said *plain drinking water.*"

"Can't be," Mila insisted. "We did the experiments. We *proved* that eggs don't float in plain water."

We agreed to keep a close eye on Bobby Solofsky. If he tried something sneaky, we'd catch him. After doing my homework, I relaxed by working on a puzzle. It was called "Mummies of Egypt." My oldest brother, Billy, walked into the living room. He was humming.

"I'm going out," he announced.

"Out *where*?" my mom asked.

Billy shrugged. "Just . . . *out.*"

My mom frowned. She squinched her nose and sniffed. "What's that smell?"

"Nothing," Billy quickly answered. "I don't smell anything. Do you smell anything, Jigsaw?"

I shook my head. I didn't smell anything. I didn't even *want* to smell anything. I

mean, who wants to smell a teenager?

My mom sniffed Billy's shirt. "Is that . . .
your father's aftershave lotion?"

"Aw, Mom," Billy complained.

"And your hair," she said, stepping back.
"It's . . . it's . . . *combed*."

Billy's face turned red. "Is not," he
protested.

"Who are you going out with?" she
asked.

"Karla."

My mom raised an eyebrow. "A girl?"

Billy messed his hair with his hands. He
fled toward the door.

"Have a nice" — the door slammed shut
— "*time*," my mom called out.

She looked at me and shook her head.

I shook mine right back.

"Teenagers," I muttered.

My dad read to me at bedtime. After he
left, I turned on my flashlight. I unfolded

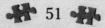

the secret code Mila had given me. Rags lay curled beside me as I stared at it.

4 marshmallows
6 coffee cups
3 coconuts
6 peppers
4 blueberries
4 tarts
1 cookie
3 spoons
3 TV dinners
2 lemons

I was starting to wish that I let Mila give me a hint after all. I closed my eyes and tried to think.

Then it hit me. The numbers! It must be something to do with the numbers. Maybe

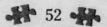

they held the secret to the code. I opened my journal and copied the list over. Then I grabbed a yellow marker.

4 marshmallows

Hmmm.

I counted to the fourth letter. I circled the "s" in marshmallows. Maybe that was it. Maybe the number was a clue. I looked at the next item on the list: 6 coffee cups. I counted six letters and circled the "e" in coffee.

I was finally getting somewhere. This was one of Mila's coolest codes yet. In the end, it read: *Secret Code.*

Not anymore!

Chapter Nine
I Hate Egg Salad

It was Tuesday. I was in the cafeteria, sitting across from Joey Pignattano.

"I hate egg salad," Joey complained.

My jaw nearly hit the table. "But Joey, you'll eat *anything*! You ate a worm once."

"I draw the line at egg salad," Joey said. He held out the sandwich. "You want it?"

"I don't even want to *look* at it," I said, holding my nose. "Take it away. It stinks."

Joey placed the sandwich on the table. I watched his eyes slide over to the garbage cans. Then back to the egg salad. Then

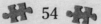

across the room to the lunch monitor —
who was staring right at him.

Joey had a problem all right. Because
today was Tuesday. His mother was lunch
monitor on Tuesdays.

"Uh-oh, trouble," I warned him. "She's
coming this way."

Joey's mom, Mrs. Pignattano, was one of
the shortest ladies I had ever seen, not
counting the Munchkins from *The Wizard of
Oz*. She wore bright red lipstick, an orange
sweatshirt, and bright yellow sweatpants.

"Joey, what's wrong with you?" she
asked. "Why aren't you eating?"

"I hate egg salad," Joey answered.

"Hate?" she repeated. "Don't say that
word. Hate is a bad word. I don't like you
using that word. Never say hate." She
waved a finger in his face.

Joey groaned. "Sorry, Momma."

Mrs. Pignattano messed his hair. "That's
a good boy," she said.

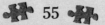 55

Joey quietly asked, "Can I say that I really, really, really *don't like* egg salad?"

Mrs. Pignattano watched Joey without expression. "Yes, Joey. You can *say* that. But first — eat your sandwich."

Joey moaned, groaned, and took a small bite. He chewed slowly, like it made his teeth hurt. All this, I thought, from a guy who once ate a worm for a dollar. I guess he really, really, really *didn't like* egg salad.

Suddenly, Mrs. Pignattano snapped her head around. She spied a crowd of boys across the room. They were playing catch with Jell-O. Mrs. Pignattano lowered her head and charged down the lane like a bowling ball. The boys scattered fast, like pins after a strike.

Joey didn't pay any attention. He just stared unhappily at his egg salad sandwich. He looked like somebody had drowned his favorite goldfish.

Chapter Ten

The Nose Knows

At long last, it was time for the great volcano show. Ms. Gleason had brought the volcano into the classroom. It almost covered the entire worktable.

Geetha began by explaining that volcanoes were really just holes in the earth's crust. "A long tunnel leads down from the top of a volcano to an underground cave," she said.

Danika Starling stood beside her. She held up a homemade poster that showed the inside of a volcano. "Hot gas from the

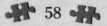 58

chamber rises up — and pushes molten rock to the surface," Geetha explained. "The red-hot rock erupts from the volcano and flows down the sides."

Now it was Helen's turn. She walked up to the volcano. "Yuck," Helen complained. "Something smells around here." Helen leaned closer to the volcano. She sniffed. "Has anyone been messing with our volcano?" she asked.

I watched everyone closely. No one said a word. But I did notice Joey Pignattano slump down in his seat. That made me wonder.

"Please go on, Helen," Ms. Gleason said.

Helen held up a small bottle with red liquid. "This is vinegar with red food coloring," Helen said. "The volcano is already filled with a small amount of sodium bi-car . . . bi-carb . . . "

"Bicarbonate," Ms. Gleason said.

"Yeah," Helen said. "What she said."

Helen poured the vinegar into the volcano. In a few seconds, the volcano began to bubble.

And bubble.

And bubble.

Higher and higher and higher.

"Is it supposed to bubble this much?" asked Ms. Gleason. She looked concerned.

Helen shook her head. "I don't think so. I only put in a little."

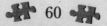

"Uh-oh," said Geetha. "I thought it was *my* job to put in the sodium bicarbonate."

"*Your* job?" asked Danika. "I thought I was supposed to do it!"

"Uh-oh, triple bubble trouble!" said Helen, staring at the erupting volcano.

More and more bubbles poured out, faster and faster. And with the bubbles came a horrible smell. I sniffed the air. It smelled familiar. But from where? I looked at Joey — he had his head buried in a book. I saw that it was upside down. Joey wasn't reading. He was hiding.

That's when I knew.

Everyone started holding their noses. Ms. Gleason opened a few windows. Poor Helen looked close to tears. "Why does our volcano stink so bad?" she wondered.

I stood up. "I have a hypothesis," I offered.

"What is it?" Helen asked.

I pulled an index card from my back pocket. I handed it to Helen. It read:

Need a Mystery Solved?
Call Jigsaw Jones
or Mila Yeh,
Private Eyes!
For a Dollar a Day,
We Make Problems Go Away!!!

Helen frowned. "I'm not paying a cent," she said.

Oh, well. It was worth a shot. "Then here's a freebie for you," I said. "It smells like eggs. Actually, it smells like egg salad."

I turned to Joey Pignattano.

Joey looked like he wanted to disappear.

"What did you *do* with that sandwich?" I asked him.

Joey's face turned red. His eyes darted

around the room. He held up his hands. "I hid it in the volcano," Joey admitted.

Everyone waited in silence. We didn't know what would happen next. Would Ms. Gleason be angry?

I heard a soft giggle. Then a snicker. It got louder. Suddenly, Ms. Gleason started laughing out loud. "Bwa-ha-ha!"

Helen laughed, too. Then Geetha and Danika. Soon everybody was laughing — even Joey. That was the end of the stinkiest, and the funniest, science project ever.

School should always be so much fun.

Chapter Eleven
A Salty Solution

Mila and I headed over to Bobby Solofsky's after school. We brought Sally-Ann Simms with us. "You'll enjoy this," I told her. "Just let us do the talking, okay?"

Sally-Ann nodded.

My finger did a few push-ups on the doorbell. The door swung open. I was shocked to see my oldest brother, Billy, standing in the doorway. "What are you doing here?" I asked him.

"Hi, worm," he said. "What are *you* doing here?"

I frowned. I saw a girl standing behind him. It was Bobby's sister, Karla.

Then it dawned on me.

Karla.

Oh, no.

I sniffed the air. Yep, it was Dad's aftershave all right. "Your new girlfriend is Karla . . . *Solofsky*?" I asked.

Billy put his hands in his pockets.

And grinned.

Yeesh.

This was bad news. I tried to figure it out in my head. If Billy fell in love with Karla, they might get married. If they got married, then Bobby Solofsky would be . . . *my relative*!

Double yeesh.

I could feel my stomach doing cartwheels.

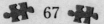 67

I didn't even like *thinking* about it. In fact, I could hardly talk.

"Hey, Bobby," Karla shouted. "Your friends are here!"

Billy put his arm around Karla. "We'll be down in the basement," he said. "Doing homework."

Finally, Bobby appeared at the door. "Hello, *Theodore*," he said. "Mila, Sally-Ann."

Mila nodded hello. Sally-Ann stuck out her tongue. I was still trying to make sense out of what I had just seen. My own brother

— my favorite, all-time best brother in the world — dating Bobby Solofsky's sister.

Triple yeesh.

"Let's get this over with, Bobby," Mila said.

We followed Bobby into his garage. There was a jar filled with water resting on a wooden box. The water was swirling around. As if it had just been stirred. A wooden spoon lay on the box. I touched it. The spoon was wet.

Why would anybody stir plain water?

Beside the jar, there was a bowl with an egg. Bobby slapped eighty-five cents on the box. "That's my end of the bet." He winked at Sally-Ann. "Look familiar? It used to be yours."

Bobby laughed.

Sally-Ann snarled.

"Are you sure you want to do this?" Bobby asked me.

"Sure, I'm sure," I replied.

 69

Bobby mumbled a few magic words, held the egg over the jar, and let it go.

The egg started to sink.

Then stopped.

It floated in the middle of the water. Just like he'd said it would.

"Ha!" Bobby shouted triumphantly. "I win! I win!"

"No, Bobby," I said. "You lose."

Bobby pulled back in surprise. "What are you talking about?"

I quickly snatched the jar from the crate. "Ordinary drinking water, right? That was the bet, wasn't it?"

"Hey, give that back," Bobby protested.

I observed it closely, like a scientist. The water looked a little cloudy. I dipped my finger into the water and tasted it.

Salty, just as I expected.

Mila stepped behind the crate. "Jigsaw, look at this." She reached down and held up a box of salt.

 70

"Cheater," Sally-Ann muttered through gritted teeth. Bobby watched helplessly as Sally-Ann Simms lifted the money off the table.

Sally-Ann tried to give me the money. I refused. "Keep it," I said. "Treat yourself to a Popsicle."

Sally-Ann grinned from ear to ear. It was the first time I'd seen her smile in days.

Bobby just stood there, scowling. "How did you know?" I tilted my head toward Mila. "She figured it out," I said. "With a little help."

"Help?" Bobby asked.

I smiled. "Tell him what your father does for a living, Mila."

"He's a science teacher," Mila said.

That left Bobby speechless. Which was exactly the way I liked him. As we walked away, Bobby called out to me, "I'll get you back one of these days, *Theodore*."

I stopped in my tracks.

I turned and looked at him.

"The name's Jigsaw," I told him. "Jigsaw Jones. Private Eye."

On the way home, Mila started singing. Sally-Ann joined her. Soon they were both hopping on the sidewalk, singing loudly:

"We all bounce on a yellow trampoline, yellow trampoline, yellow trampoline!"

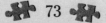

Oh, brother.

Anyway, I was glad. It was another mystery solved. No surprise there. After all, it's what any good scientist would have predicted!